A Christmas Tree
for Pyn

For John and the pups

with all my love and laughter

PHILOMEL BOOKS
A division of Penguin Young Readers Group.
Published by The Penguin Group.
Penguin Group (USA) Inc., 375 Hudson Street,
New York, NY 10014, U.S.A.
Penguin Group (Canada), 90 Eglinton Avenue East,
Suite 700, Toronto, Ontario M4P 2Y3, Canada
(a division of Pearson Penguin Canada Inc.).
Penguin Books Ltd, 80 Strand, London WC2R 0RL, England.
Penguin Ireland, 25 St. Stephen's Green, Dublin 2, Ireland (a division of Penguin Books Ltd).
Penguin Group (Australia), 250 Camberwell Road, Camberwell, Victoria 3124, Australia (a division of
Pearson Australia Group Pty Ltd).
Penguin Books India Pvt Ltd, 11 Community Centre, Panchsheel Park, New Delhi - 110 017, India.
Penguin Group (NZ), 67 Apollo Drive, Rosedale, North Shore 0632, New Zealand (a division of Pearson New Zealand Ltd).
Penguin Books (South Africa) (Pty) Ltd, 24 Sturdee Avenue, Rosebank, Johannesburg 2196, South Africa.
Penguin Books Ltd, Registered Offices: 80 Strand, London WC2R 0RL, England.

Published simultaneously in Canada. Manufactured in China by South China Printing Co. Ltd.
Edited by Jill Santopolo. Design by Semadar Megged. Text set in 16-point Zapf Humanist 601 BT. The artwork is rendered in pencil and gouache on 140 lb. d'Arches rough watercolor paper.

Library of Congress Cataloging-in-Publication Data
Dunrea, Olivier. A Christmas tree for Pyn / Olivier Dunrea. p. cm. Summary: Little Pyn finally persuades her gruff father to find the perfect Christmas tree in the snowy forest and, after bringing it home, decorates it with him.
[1. Christmas trees—Fiction. 2. Fathers and daughters—Fiction. 3. Christmas—Fiction.] I. Title. PZ7.D922Ch 2011 [E]—dc22
ISBN 978-0-399-24506-0
10 9 8 7 6 5 4 3 2 1

A Christmas Tree for Pyn

Olivier Dunrea

Philomel Books
An Imprint of Penguin Group (USA) Inc.

On top of a steep, craggy mountain lived a bear of a man named Oother and his small daughter, Pyn.

Oother was a big, gruff man. He had a loud, booming voice, large, rough hands, and a bristly black beard.

Pyn was a small, soft girl. She had a quiet, gentle voice, tiny, smooth hands, and two bunches of hair bouncing off either side of her head.

Every morning Pyn crawled out of bed and made a hearty breakfast for Oother.

"Good morning, Papa," Pyn said.

"My name is Oother," said Oother.

"Good morning, Oother," said Pyn.

"Umphf," said Oother.

Oother loved his daughter very much. But he was a bearlike mountain man who did not soften for anyone. Not even Pyn.

He ate his breakfast of hot porridge, honey, and steaming baked bread.

It was late December. The trees stood dark against the sky and the white snow.

Oother pulled on his heavy fur coat and fur boots and set off into the woods. While he was gone, Pyn cleared away and washed the dishes. She swept the floor, made the beds, and fluffed the pillows. Pyn poked the fire and added more wood. She wanted the cottage to be snug and warm when Oother returned from a cold day's work in the woods.

At the end of the day, when the wind whistled around the cottage, Oother returned home. He stamped the snow off his fur boots and burst into the cottage, slamming the heavy door behind him.

Pyn had set the table and ladled out a large bowl of steaming soup for Oother. She set a small bowl for herself.

"Good evening, Papa," said Pyn.

"My name is Oother," said Oother.

"Good evening, Oother," said Pyn.

"Umphf," said Oother.

And with a grunt he began to eat the hot soup.

Pyn watched him eat in silence.

"Oother," said Pyn, "Christmas is coming. Do you think we could have a Christmas tree this year?"

"No Christmas tree," said Oother.

He continued to eat.

Oother was a big, gruff man who did not like to speak when he ate.

"I could go with you into the woods to find the perfect tree," said Pyn. "And we could decorate it like the people in the village do."

"No Christmas tree," said Oother.

"It wouldn't have to be a very big tree," continued Pyn. "I could make decorations and we could have a real Christmas for the first time."

Oother put down his spoon and wiped his bristly beard and mustache with the back of his hand. He looked at his tiny daughter, whose eyes danced brightly in the firelight.

How very much like her mother she is, he thought.

"We'll see," said Oother.

And with that he crawled into the large wooden bed and fell asleep.

Pyn sat and stared into the fire, imagining what it would be like to have a real Christmas tree in the cottage. She knew it would not be as beautiful as the decorated trees she had seen in the village. She had been saving bits of odds and ends that she had found in the woods that might make a fir tree into a real Christmas tree.

On Christmas Eve morning Oother ate his thick porridge and honey and drank a large mug of strong coffee. Pyn ate her porridge and with hopeful eyes watched the huge man.

Oother pushed away from the table. He pulled on his fur boots, bundled himself into his coat and hat, thrust his hands into thick mittens, and picked up his heavy ax.

Pyn held her breath and waited.

Without a word Oother stomped out of the cottage.

Pyn jumped up from her stool and quickly pulled on her fur boots. She became tangled in her fur coat and scarf as she scrambled to put them on. Her fur hat slid down over her eyes. In her rush to get ready she fell over and sat hard on the floor.

"I'll surprise Oother," Pyn said to herself. "I'll find the perfect Christmas tree and will cut it down myself and bring it home. He did say 'We'll see.'"

Pyn pushed open the heavy door.

She struggled through the snow, stopping now and then to catch her breath.

Finding the perfect Christmas tree is hard work, she thought.

Suddenly, a heavy clump of snow fell from a thick branch above and buried the small girl under its weight.

Before Pyn knew what happened, Oother scooped her up by the scruff of her neck with one hand. He held her at arm's length and shook the snow off her.

"What were you doing out here in the cold?" he said. "A big snowstorm is coming."

"I wanted to find the perfect Christmas tree," said Pyn. "And surprise you."

Oother stared hard at his daughter as she shivered in the cold.

In one swift movement he swept her off her feet and placed her on his shoulders.

Together they trudged into the dark woods.

"Papa," said Pyn.

"My name's Oother," said Oother.

"Oother," said Pyn. "Where will we find a Christmas tree?"

"You'll see," said Oother.

They came to an open meadow at the edge of the woods.

"Christmas trees!" exclaimed Pyn.

"Umphf," said Oother.

"But how will we find just the right one?" asked Pyn.

She could barely see through the thickly falling snow.

And then she saw it. The perfect Christmas tree.

"There!" she cried. "Over there."

Oother tromped to where she pointed and stopped. Pyn squirmed on his shoulders with excitement.

"That's the tree," she said. "That's our Christmas tree!"

Oother hefted her off his shoulders and dropped her in the snow. Pyn disappeared from sight. Oother reached down and pulled her from the deep snowdrift. He plopped her on top of a large gray boulder.

"Don't move," he said.

Before he chopped down the fir tree, Oother and Pyn bowed their heads and gave thanks to the fir tree for allowing them to cut it down.

In three swift chops Oother felled the tree. He grabbed Pyn by the arm and tossed her back onto his shoulders. He gripped his large ax in one hand and grasped the trunk of the Christmas tree with the other.

Father and daughter headed back to the cottage.

Pyn could not take her eyes off the fir tree.

My first Christmas tree! she thought.

The cottage was nearly buried under the snow. Thin blue smoke rose from the chimney and vanished in the thickly falling snow.

Oother stamped his big fur boots outside the door. The snow was falling harder. The mountaintop was shrouded in whiteness.

"Oh, Papa!" cried Pyn. "It's the most perfect Christmas tree."

"My name's Oother," said Oother.

Oother found an old tub and filled it with water. He placed the fir tree in it and braced it with stones so that it stood tall and straight, just as it had done in the snowy meadow.

Pyn clapped her hands and danced in front of the fir tree.

"It's beautiful!" she said in a hushed voice. "Just beautiful."

"Now you have a Christmas tree," said Oother.

"Oh, but it's not finished yet," said Pyn. "We have to decorate it."

"Umphf," said Oother.

Pyn dashed across the room and opened the wooden chest at the foot of her bed. From inside she took out a collection of all the things she had found in the woods. First, she took out abandoned birds' nests, some with unhatched eggs that had dried out but were still unbroken. Pyn reached into the wooden chest again and pulled out a number of old wasps' nests with their intricate honeycomb pattern.

She pulled out several small hornets' nests that she had carefully wrapped in paper. Large acorns tumbled onto the floor from a small bag. In another bag she had collected bright red berries. Then she took out her most prized treasures of all—birds' feathers that she had gleaned during her walks in the woods.

The feathers were of all sizes and colors: shimmering blues and greens, vibrant reds and yellows, and glossy blacks and purples.

One by one she carried all the treasures and placed them carefully on the floor in front of the fir tree.

"Now we can decorate the Christmas tree!" she announced.

Oother silently watched as Pyn bustled about the tree, carefully placing the nests so that the eggs could be seen. She tied bits of string to the tops of the hornets' nests and hung them from the ends of the branches. She tucked the wasps' nests so that they shone pale against the dark green of the fir tree. Pyn hung the acorns all over the tree.

She sat on the floor and, with needle in hand, strung the berries onto a long piece of sturdy thread.

Oother held her high so that she could hang her ornaments on the topmost branches. He helped her wrap the berry garland around the Christmas tree, starting at the top and carefully working their way down to the bottom.

"Now the feathers!" Pyn said.

Together they placed the brightly colored feathers among the branches until the fir tree glistened with color.

"It's beautiful!" she said. "A real Christmas tree."

Oother stared at the tree in amazement. It *was* beautiful.

"Wait," he said and stomped down the stone steps into the cold cellar. Pyn could hear him rummaging around below.

Oother clumped up the stone steps into the light. He held a small package.

"For your Christmas tree," he said. "It belonged to your mother."

He handed the small bundle to Pyn.

Pyn stared at it.

"What is it?" she asked.

"Open it," said Oother.

Pyn slowly unwrapped the package. Inside was the most beautiful bird she had ever seen. It was made from real feathers, with two black beads for eyes and two long feathers streaming from behind.

Pyn stared at Oother.

"I made it for your mother," Oother said softly. "For the top of the Christmas tree."

Pyn carefully held the bird in her hands.

"It's the most beautiful bird I've ever seen," Pyn whispered.

Oother gently lifted her and Pyn placed the bird at the very top of the tree.

Oother set her back on the floor and the two of them gazed in wonder at the Christmas tree.

In the firelight the feathers of the bird glistened and shimmered.

"A real Christmas tree," said Pyn.

"A real Christmas tree," said Oother.

"Thank you, Oother!" said Pyn.

"My name's Papa," Oother said.

"Thank you, Papa!" cried Pyn, throwing her arms around his neck.

The fire burned low. Pyn yawned.

Oother quietly carried Pyn to her bed.

"Good night, daughter," said Papa. "Merry Christmas."